Chrome and Chaos
A Gaya Story

Colin J. Fantry

www.ten16press.com - Waukesha, WI

Chrome and Chaos: A Gaya Story
Copyrighted © 2021 Colin J. Fantry
ISBN Paperback 9781645382713
ISBN Ebook 9781645382737
First Edition

Chrome and Chaos: A Gaya Story
by Colin J. Fantry

Cover design by Jayden Ellsworth

For information, please contact:

www.ten16press.com
Waukesha, WI

I dedicate this book to aspiring writers and artists of all kinds.
Make what you love.
There's no better time than the present.

Protectors of the Weak,
Students of the World

The wind was blowing hard that morning. It was early Spring, and the Winter chill was still on its way out. The woman walking through the woods pulled her cloak tighter around her, though her companion seemed unfazed by it. The dew covering the forest floor was starting to seep in through a small hole in her leather boots, making the chill just that little bit more biting. Her seemingly weather-proof companion turned to look at her. "I know it's cold and all, but you haven't let your hood down at all since I've met you."

Her heart began to beat a little faster at the mention of her hood. She had hoped he wouldn't notice. "Let me guess," he continued, "you're an Elf, right?"

She sighed, and half-heartedly replied, "A Half-Elf."

The man let out a short laugh, startling his Half-

Elven companion. "Well then I was half right! I know that sometimes we humans can get suspicious of the other races, but personally I don't care. You aren't some sort of demon, you're just a person with pointy ears."

The Half-Elf sighed again, but this time with relief. She let her hood down to reveal her pointed ears, and then, suddenly remembering the cold, pulled it back up. "I do not think that you told me your name," she said quietly.

Her companion laughed again, louder this time. "Well, I guess I forgot! You weren't exactly one for conversation. My name's Leon. Now it's only fair that you tell me yours."

"My name is Gwenraele Naeran," she replied, a bit more confidence pushing its way into her voice.

"That's quite a mouthful. I think I'll call you Gwen."

Gwen frowned slightly at this, though she tried not to show it. She had never been all that fond of nicknames, though she wasn't going to argue with her superior. When she turned to look at Leon, he was smiling at her, though it didn't seem to reach all the way to his eyes. He was tall, though not so tall as to stand out. He had a rough face, with a looping scar on his cheek that reminded Gwen of a wisp of smoke. Leon was likely nearing middle age, given the slight tinges of grey at the edges of his unkempt, shaggy black hair. He didn't have a beard, though he likely hadn't shaved in a few days, as his whiskers were on the edge of turning into one.

Gwen was slightly shorter than Leon, and with her cloak wrapped around her she looked rather unassuming. Beneath that cloak, however, she was surprisingly muscular. She had undergone intense physical training in addition to schooling during her time in the Guild College, and it showed. Her long brown hair was tied into a tight bun. Her bright green eyes seemed ravenous, always scanning the environment around her. Whenever she looked at someone, it seemed as though she were trying to read them like a book. It was this very look that she was unwittingly giving Leon, seemingly trying to suck out his story through her eyes.

Gwen was suddenly shaken from her thoughts, as Leon began to speak. "So, this is your first real mission with the Guild, huh?"

"Yes. I graduated just a month ago, and they decided I was ready for my first assignment."

"Well then, let me offer you a warm welcome to The Guild of Walls and Tomes! I hope you find the work fulfilling. I've always loved…"

The warm expression on Leon's face suddenly dropped away, and he held his hand up to signal a stop.

As she did so, Gwen noticed a rustling coming from the brush on their right. She put her hand on the hilt of her shortsword, bracing herself for a confrontation. Suddenly, a boar charged out from the woods, tusks bearing down on the two travellers. Gwen dove out of the way of the creature, rolling to her knees and drawing her shortsword. Leon did the same, pulling his greataxe from its sheath on his back. The boar missed both of them, and it slid to a halt at the edge of the footpath. It turned around to face the two travellers, its breath turning to steam in the cold morning air. Leon turned to look at Gwen and nodded his head, a look Gwen took to mean "Follow my lead."

Leon whistled at the enraged creature before them, trying to goad it into charging. The boar, eyes filled with a primal, murderous rage, turned and charged at Leon. Without missing a beat, Leon charged in turn, and, using the boar's back as a springboard, vaulted over the boar. If the boar was capable of feeling surprised, it certainly felt it, though not for very long. Being so focused on Leon, it had failed to notice the tree directly behind him, and charged headlong into the solid oak. Before the concussed creature had time to recover, Gwen and Leon took the chance to make a charge of their own. Gwen thrust the point of her blade into the boar's exposed flank, and Leon brought his greataxe down on its neck. The creature fell limp to the ground, and breathed one last, shuddering breath, before falling silent.

Gwen pulled her sword from the beast and smirked. "Hm," she remarked, "We did not even need to use our Alterations."

"Well, don't say that too soon," Leon murmured. His voice seemed strained and in pain.

Gwen turned to look at her companion, and saw him kneeling on the ground holding his leg, blood flowing from a wound in his right shin. "The damned thing got me good on my way up. I don't suppose you specialize in healing magic?" Leon tried to smile at this last remark, but it quickly faded in the wake of pain.

"No, not quite, but I should be able to patch it up." Gwen had taken a few first aid classes in her time at the College, so she knew enough to at least bandage the wound. She reached into the small pouch on her belt, and pulled out a roll of cloth. She bent down and began to wrap up Leon's shin. The wound was deep, but not life threatening.

Leon grimaced as she tightened the wrap, focusing his gaze away from his wounded leg. "Thanks. I'd do this myself, but I'm not too good with blood." He tried to laugh, but it more so turned into a gasp of pain as Gwen pulled the wrap tight and tied it up.

Gwen helped Leon to his feet. He was able to walk on his own just fine, though she noticed he had a very slight limp. "That's what I get for trying to be stylish, I suppose." He laughed again, quietly this time, and Gwen giggled behind her hand.

They started on their way again, and Leon turned to Gwen and asked, "So I know you don't do healing, but what kind of Alteration do you do?"

"Illusions mostly," she stated matter of factly.

"Ooh, an Illusionist! I haven't seen many of those as of late. Most people seem so enamored with battle Alterations. They like the flashiness and the straightforward fighting, though I find that utility magics, like illusions, are more practical for everyday use. I'm a specialist with fire Alterations myself. It's the kind of Alteration that I came to naturally, but I have to admit that a part of me is jealous of the Healers and Illusionists. I find their work to be so much more creative than just throwing one of the four elements at a guy until he can't move anymore."

Gwen didn't respond, staring at the ground in front of her. Leon cocked his head to one side, and asked "Is there something interesting about that dirt that I missed?"

This startled Gwen out of her thoughts, and, flustered, she said, "O-oh, no, no, it's just…"

"Nervous about your first assignment, huh?"

"Y-yes, yes, I suppose so."

"Don't be. This is the sort of assignment we get all the time. Some local villagers disappear, someone claims to have seen a monster, and so we get called in to clean it up. It's probably just some bear that someone mistook for a monster in the dark. We take care of the 'monster,' the town thanks us, and we get paid. Clean and simple."

Gwen took a deep breath and replied, "Yes, yes you're probably right." She still looked nervous, but Leon's words of assurance seemed to have had at least some effect.

Leon, still trying to make conversation, said, "I'm just glad the town isn't too far away from the Capital. Makes it easier for us, less baggage and all."

Gwen nodded, though it was clear she wasn't paying close attention, once again lost in her thoughts. Leon grinned, shook his head, and decided that trying to get her to talk wasn't worth the trouble.

It was a few hours more before the pair emerged from the woods and onto a grassy plain. Without the trees and foliage obscuring their view, the travellers could see their destination ahead of them, a town named Wildepeak.

The town was near the main thoroughfare to Solace, the Capital of Acrium, and so functioned as a resting place for those travelling to and from the city. It also served as an outpost for those hunting and trapping in the nearby woods. It got its name from the large hill in the center of town, at the top of which sat a grand mansion. As they got closer, Leon turned to Gwen, and said, "Look, I may not judge you for what you look like, but these village folk are prone to being suspicious of outsiders, especially ones that don't look like them. I'd recommend you pull your hood back over your ears. It'll make things a lot easier."

Gwen was used to hiding her Elven heritage, and so pulled her cloak's hood back over her head, having let it down as the day warmed. The two entered Wildepeak from a back road, and made their way towards the hill at the center of the town. As they went, the sounds of the villagers going about their business filled the air. The sounds of bartering, of shouting arguments, and of hawkers trying to get the attention of passers by replaced the quiet calm of the forest they had been travelling through. The smell of baked goods and cooking meat wafted from the open door of the local tavern. The two cloaked strangers received a few sidelong glances from the locals, but not much beyond that.

It was nearing midday by the time Gwen and Leon reached the foot of the great hill. A stonework wall surrounded much of the hill, with an ornate iron gate at its center. Two guards stood at either side of the gate, simple spears in hand. As the travellers approached the gate, the guards crossed their spears in front of the gate, and the taller of the two asked in an almost bored tone, "State your business."

Leon looked the guards up and down, seemingly deciding how to respond, then said "We're the representatives of The Guild of Walls and Tomes. Your mayor requested our presence."

At the mention of the Guild, the guards instinctively took a step back. Then, after having collected himself, the second guard said, "You may enter. The Mayor is expecting you."

The guards pushed open the gates, gesturing for Gwen and Leon to move through. As they did so, the two guards quickly closed the gates behind them. Gwen, taken aback by their reactions, asked Leon, "Why did they seem so scared of us? Do they not know we're here to help them?"

Leon sighed slightly and, with a tired expression, replied, "Most people outside of the big cities aren't too used to seeing Alterers like us, and, frankly, they're afraid of us. They think we're a bad omen. I can't exactly blame them."

Gwen was puzzled a bit by this answer, but decided against pressing any further. The two Alterers made their way up the walkway towards the mansion. The yard surrounding the mansion was filled with beautiful flowers and sculpted shrubbery, only slightly undercut by the fact that everything was slanted, making one feel as though they were always just on the verge of falling over. The mansion itself was large relative to the town below, but was nothing compared to what could be found in bigger cities. It was a two-story affair, made of wood from the nearby forest. The second floor windows shot blinding reflections of the sun into the eyes of whoever happened to be unlucky enough to look up, and a stone entryway held up by ornately carved stone pillars clashed stylistically with the rest of the wooden house. As Gwen and Leon climbed the stone steps towards the entryway, they were greeted by a well-dressed elderly man. He silently opened the door and motioned for them to follow.

Compared to the gaudy outside of the mansion, the inside was surprisingly sparse. An animal hide rug covered the entryway, and a simple dining table could be seen in the adjoining room. To their right, a narrow staircase led towards the second floor. As the travellers stepped inside, the well dressed man, who they presumed to be a servant, said, "The master awaits you in his study. It is the center door you will see immediately as you reach the second floor. I will take your cloaks."

At this, Leon began to take off his cloak, but shot a look of concern towards Gwen. Gwen simply nodded her head at him. Then, she whispered something inaudible under her breath, put her hands beneath the hood of her cloak, and pushed back the hood to reveal what looked to be unremarkable human ears. Leon smiled, this time from his eyes as well as his mouth. The servant took their cloaks and journeyed deeper into the house, leaving Gwen and Leon to themselves.

Gwen turned to Leon and explained, "I am just going to project the illusion into the minds of everyone I see, even you. It makes my job simpler. I do not usually like to waste my energy like this, but as long as I do not have to keep up the illusion for long, I will be fine."

"Now that's what I was talking about! Utility magic is so useful for situations like this. It's not like I could've used fire to make your ears disappear!" Leon's passion for magic was written all over his face, but as Gwen motioned towards the stairs in front of them, he quickly collected himself and led the way up the stairs.

The second floor was as sparse as the first, with nothing to cover the floors nor anything hanging up on the walls. The stairway opened into a hallway, with three doors in total: one at either end of the hall, and one in the center. Leon reached out towards the middle door and knocked twice. "Enter!" rang out a nasally voice from within.

The room that they entered was enormous, likely taking up most of the second floor. The walls were covered floor to ceiling with bookshelves, except for the fireplace in the center of the far wall. Above the fireplace was a large portrait of a young, fit man standing with his foot atop a bear, recently killed. It was not that young man that sat at the small, lone desk in the center of the room, however. The man was in his later middle-age, bald on the top of his head but with a long moustache to compensate. He was quite large around the waist, apparently quite the gourmand. He wore what would have been elegant clothes, if it weren't for the combination of candle wax and grease that stained them. As Leon and Gwen entered the room, the rotund man stood up and moved towards them with his hand outstretched. "Hello Alterers! It is so good to meet you! My name is Sir Philoman Neiper."

The mayor's hand was sweaty, and he smelled of candle wax and stale cheese. Leon was seemingly unphased, but

Gwen had to stifle the urge to make a face as she shook his hand. The mayor took a step back and said, "Did my procession meet you at the town's entrance? I requested they meet you so that you might be celebrated!"

Leon quickly replied "Oh, don't worry about that! We took a shortcut through the Mistyoak Woods, so we ended up taking back roads to get here."

At this, the mayor frowned for a moment and said, seemingly to himself, "Oh, then I really ought to call them back. They may still be out there..."

Growing slightly impatient, Gwen quietly asked, "Um, pardon me Mr. Mayor, but would you mind telling us what it is you require from us?"

The mayor, startled from his thoughts of abandoned processions, replied, "Oh, oh yes of course! You see, a few hunters have gone missing a few miles south of the city. Now, ordinarily this wouldn't be that unusual, but these were some of the stronger hunters that frequent this town. They wouldn't have disappeared without a fight, but my search parties haven't found so much as a trace of them. Additionally, some of the nearby farmers claim to have seen monsters skulking through their fields at night. If it were simply one of these claims in isolation, I would have paid it little mind, but the combination of the two has me, as well as the rest of the town, a bit on edge. Therefore, I requested your expertise. All I need you to do is to check around where those hunters were hunting before they disappeared, and verify whether or not magic or monsters are at play. If you follow the road south of town for an hour or so, then turn right you'll see a trail in the woods. Follow that and you'll find the clearing where the hunters disappeared. Oh, but uh, there's no need for any special hurry. Feel free to rest here for the night and set out in the morning. I will be covering your expenses at the inn."

"Well, thank you very much Mr. Mayor," Leon said, once again putting on a fake grin. "We'll head over to the inn right now. We'll let you know if we need anything else."

At this, Leon quickly turned around and motioned for Gwen to follow. She hurried to catch up as he briskly walked down the stairs and out the door, taking his cloak from the servant waiting for them at the bottom of the stairs. Gwen followed suit, passing her hands over her ears once she had her cloak back, pulling the hood back up over her head to cover her re-pointed ears. As they passed through the front gate and out into the town, Gwen turned to her companion and asked, "Why did you leave so suddenly?"

"The man annoyed me," Leon said tersely. "I've seen

his kind a hundred times. He's a spoiled child too scared to do anything himself. Now I'm sure it's just gonna be some bear." Leon laughed humorlessly to himself. "Ah well, at least we get paid, right newby?"

Gwen wasn't sure how to respond, and so she just nodded. They walked in silence until they reached the village's one inn. Leon walked up to the young woman at the counter, and whispered something that Gwen couldn't quite make out. The woman then pulled out two keys, and said, "The rooms are all yours. There's a tavern across the street whenever you want to eat."

Leon again motioned for Gwen to follow, as he quickly walked up the set of stairs leading to the guest rooms. "This room's yours," he said, pounding it with his fist as he passed. "And this one's mine." He tossed one of the sets of keys to Gwen, who, unprepared for the keys to be thrown at her, tossed them up a few times before finally catching them. Leon then unlocked his room, went in, and slammed the door behind him.

Gwen, a little shaken, quietly unlocked the door to her room and stepped inside. It was relatively small, with only a bed and a chair in the far corner, but it was enough. Gwen took off her cloak and flung it on the corner chair. Then, reaching into the small pack she had been carrying on her back, she took out an old book, sat on the bed, and began to read.

Hours went by before Gwen even realized it. The sun was setting when she heard a knock at her door. "Yes?"

"It's Leon. Do you want to get something to eat?"

"Um, sure - I-I mean yes."

"Great! Do you plan on opening the door?"

Flustered, Gwen shot up from the bed, grabbed her cloak from the chair, and went out to meet Leon. He seemed in a better mood than he had been when they arrived, and the two of them went over to The Whispering Arrow Tavern across the street. As the two sat down, Leon cocked his head to one side quizzically, and asked, "Are you old enough to drink?"

Slightly annoyed, Gwen shot back, "I'm nearly 27, of course I'm old enough to drink!"

"Alright, alright. I just didn't know if Half-Elves aged as fast as humans or not."

"It's fine. I don't - er - I do not plan on drinking while on an assignment."

"Do you always talk so formally?"

At this Gwen looked down at the table, trying to hide the red rising to her face beneath her cloak.

Seeing this, Leon said, "Well, if we're going to be working together, I'd at least like you to be comfortable around me. Let's play a little game. For every question

I ask you, you ask me a question. Whoever refuses to answer first loses. I already asked you my first question, and your face was answer enough, so now it's your turn."

Gwen took a moment to collect her thoughts, then asked, "How long have you been working for the Guild?"

"Easy, 16 years. Why did you join the Guild?"

"To help others."

Leon smirked. "Oho, quite the noble goal. Your turn."

"Why did you join?"

"My my, stealing questions now, are we? I joined because I was too curious for my own good. I wanted to learn, hence the 'Tomes' part of 'The Guild of Walls and Tomes.' I ended up doing more than just some research projects though." Leon paused for a moment, clearly thinking back on his time in the Guild. "Anyhow, time to think of a question for you. Let's see… Oh! What was your time at the Guild College like?"

Gwen instinctively shuddered at the mention of the College. "Not exactly what I had been expecting. I was hoping to just do some Alteration training. Instead, I ended up doing a bit of everything. Hell, now I know how to use a sword. I never thought I'd be using a sword. To be honest, it was mainly just a lot of training and studying."

"Not exactly the type for parties, huh?"

Gwen raised an eyebrow at Leon. "What do you think?"

At this, Leon burst out laughing, surprising and confusing Gwen in the process. "Hah, I think that's the first joke I've heard you say! Congrats!"

Gwen bristled a bit at this assertion, and decided to go for the throat. "That scar on your cheek, where did you get it from?"

Leon's expression did not change, though the mirth seemed to somewhat drain from his eyes. "Well, it looks like we have ourselves a winner."

Gwen smirked, a sense of satisfaction flowing through her. The two ate their meals with polite, though slightly less confrontational, conversation. Gwen decided to abstain from alcohol, choosing instead to take tea, but Leon was not of the same mindset. It was dark when they decided to return to the inn, or more specifically when Gwen decided to take Leon back to the inn.

The road was lit by simple candle lanterns placed every few feet along it. As the two exited the tavern, the wind blew the hood of Gwen's cloak back, revealing the trademark pointed ears hidden beneath. Before she had a chance to pull the hood back up, a man, likely on his way home from a night of strong spirits, caught a glimpse of her elvish ears. He scowled at her, and growled out, "So, you must be one a them Alterers everyone's been talkin' 'bout. Well, you ain't so special. I bet yer ears would go fer a mighty good price to some collector."

Leon took a step forward, but Gwen held out his hand to stop her inebriated companion. She closed her eyes for a moment, concentrating. Then, whispering under her breath and making small swift movements with her hands, she opened her eyes and stared directly at the man who had threatened her. Her eyes glowed a bright red, and from behind her, a shadowy figure with those same glowing red eyes arose. The features were impossible to make out in the darkness, but it was easily 7 or 8 feet tall. Both sets of piercing crimson eyes locked squarely on the now quivering drunk. The voice that emerged from Gwen was low and resonant, seeming to echo not only through the streets around them, but through the very mind of the man. "Oh, you wish to challenge me? You certainly are a brave little man. It's a shame that there's nothing worth taking from you as a trophy, though I do wonder how your soul will taste."

At this, the last vestiges of the man's courage failed him, and he ran away from the glowing Half-Elf and her shadowy companion as fast as he could manage. Once he was gone, the figure behind Gwen melted back into shadows, and she fell to one knee, exhausted by the effort of creating it. She laughed quietly, and said, "I made sure that only the three of us could see any of those illusions. If he tries to tell anyone, they're going to think he's lost it."

Leon, still addled by the alcohol, stammered out, "I-I'm sorry, but what just happened?"

Gwen sighed, and, with a tinge of exasperation creeping into her voice, said, "We can talk about it tomorrow. You should just get some sleep."

The two slept soundly that night. Gwen was the first to rise, and went to knock on Leon's door. The man who answered certainly looked like Leon, but the voice that escaped him seemed like that of a dying man. "Look, just, just give me a few minutes, alright? My head is absolutely killing me."

"And you laughed at me for not drinking on the job."

Leon glared at Gwen, and, massaging the bridge of his nose with his thumb and forefinger, muttered, "Just meet me downstairs in 30 minutes, alright?"

"If you can even make it that long."

In response, Leon slammed the door loudly in Gwen's face, followed by a soft groan of pain from within.

An hour later, Leon and Gwen were out in the early morning cold. The two followed the mayor's instructions and, about an hour and a half later found themselves in a circular clearing in the Mistyoak Woods. Leon surveyed the clearing for a moment, sighed, then started to turn around. Shocked, Gwen turned to him and asked "Where are you going? We need to check for signs of monsters."

"There's nothing here. Monsters always leave behind signs when they inhabit an area. Monsters are beings of pure magical energy. They scour the land wherever they go. Their very presence can cause plant life to decay, and, if there was one nesting nearby, there's no way the forest would look this healthy. There are no monsters around here, just some unlucky hunters, some gossiping villagers, and a lazy mayor. I really don't feel like dealing with this right now. I'm tired and my head is killing me. Let's just collect our pay and get out of this damned backwater."

"Well, I want to be sure. Shouldn't we just check a little bit at least?"

Relenting, Leon sighed, "Fine. We'll look around a bit, but I'm telling you, there are no monsters around here."

Gwen found this answer to be good enough, and began looking around the clearing, trying to find anything that seemed out of place. Leon, for his part, tried to put on an act of searching for clues as well, but anyone could see that his heart wasn't in it. Then, out of the corner of her eye, Gwen saw something shift slightly deeper in the woods. At first she thought it was a trick of the mind, but then it happened again. It was like the trunks of the oak trees suddenly shifted in the wind, and then were solid again. She decided to get a closer look. As she grew nearer to the strange, shifting oak trees, she reached out her hand to touch them, and her hand passed right through them without any sort of resistance. She put her hand in and out of these nonexistent trees a few times, just to assure herself that she wasn't imagining things, and then turned to Leon. "Hey Leon, I think I found something."

"What do you mean you 'found something'?"

"Well, I guess it would be more accurate to say I didn't find something, but… oh just come here."

As Leon approached, one eyebrow raised in apprehension, Gwen once again put her hand through the oak tree. At this Leon's second eyebrow rose to find his first. "Huh, I guess you did find something. Glad I had you around for this. I would have never seen that illusion magic."

"See, that's the weird thing. This doesn't feel like a normal illusion Alteration. It's hard for me to describe, but this feels, oh, I don't know, different somehow? Does that make any sense?"

"Not really, but I'll take your word for it."

Leon took a few steps forward then, suddenly, stuck his head through the illusionary tree, much to Gwen's surprise. "Huh," he declared, "it's pretty dark in there."

"Do you normally go around sticking your head into random places?"

"It's worked out fine for me so far." At this Leon reached into the small sack he had been carrying and took out a torch. He held the rag covered end of the torch near his hand and, after a couple of snaps of his fingers, lit it with a spark. Turning to Gwen, he said "Well come on, then," and walked into the phony tree. Gwen, suddenly alone in the forest, quickly followed suit.

The place that the two found themselves in was cold, colder than the spring morning from which they came. The lively forest to which they had grown accustomed gave way to a narrow chrome room with a curved ceiling. In fact, every surface in the room was covered in metal, which glowed in the torchlight. Straight ahead of them, a set of metal stairs led further down into the iron tunnel. Leon led the way, with Gwen only a few steps behind. As they went deeper into the tunnel, the sounds of the forest grew more and more faint, until all they could hear was the echo of their footfalls on the cold hard ground. From the bottom of the stairwell, a faint blue light broke through the darkness. When Gwen and Leon reached the source of the light, they found the walls were covered floor to ceiling in runes, each glowing in that soft blue light. Leon traced the runes with his finger, eyeing them with a mix of curiosity and apprehension. "How did we not know about this?" he muttered to himself.

"Leon, do you know where we are?" Stirred from his thoughts, Leon glanced backwards at Gwen. "Oh, I suppose they wouldn't have taught you about this kind of thing yet. It's above your paygrade."

"If you're trying to make me feel better, it's not working."

"Remember how I told you I joined the Guild to learn? Well, the creators of this place were one of my research projects. They have a lot of different names depending on where in Gaya you are, but the name I like the best is 'The Criterions.' How much do you know about Gaya's history?"

"I mean, I know about the founding of the Three Nations, the Great Sundering…"

"No, that's not quite what I meant." At this, Leon turned and started down the passageway. "Well, I guess now is as good a time as any for a history lesson." Gwen followed him, lagging a few paces behind. She hugged her arms to her chest, both to ward off the cold and to ward off the fear that was rising in her heart.

"A very, very long time ago," Leon began, "before there was a Gaya, there was Vaeriel, Mother of Chaos, creator of magic, and the first goddess. It was thanks to her that the rest of the gods came into being, and the gods, together with Vaeriel, created Gaya. All of the gods crafted life on Gaya, but the creatures that Vaeriel made, beasts of pure chaos, consumed everything in their path. In order to allow life to thrive on Gaya, the rest of the gods all banded together and sealed Variel away in another plane of existence, so that she couldn't affect this world. This is what we call the First Age. In the Second Age, the gods, despite being weakened by their sealing of Vaeriel, made new life for Gaya. The race of people that dominated the Second Age were what made this place, the Criterions. But because Vaeriel could no longer reach Gaya, the Criterions could not use Alterations. Instead, they used Gaya's natural materials to make wonders that you or I might compare to magic. But the Criterions grew prideful. They wanted to be the most powerful beings on this plane, and so sought to destroy the gods. The gods, weakened as they were, knew that they could not defeat the Criterions on their own. In order to save themselves, they struck a deal with Vaeriel, and together they defeated the Criterions. This marked the end of the

Second Age. These ruins are all that's left of their once mighty empire. No one really knows what happened to them after they were defeated, and that's where I come in. I was tasked with investigating where the Criterions went after their war with the gods. I've done plenty of research into them, but I've never actually been in one of their ruins before."

Gwen, still uneasy, asked "Are we in any danger?"

"Probably not. I doubt anything would be living down here. This place feels really foreign to natural life. If I were a beast, I'd steer clear of this place."

This did little to assuage Gwen's fears, but she kept on. The passageway seemed to stretch on and on, until finally the two of them saw an entryway at the end of the hall. It opened into a large square room. Light emanated from a hole in the ceiling, colder in hue than any torch. In contrast to the hall they had just come from, the walls and floor were made of a white stone brick. The only other entrance to the room was another open doorway on the right wall, and the same kind of light that shone in the room lit the next hallway as well. In the center of the room lay a table, on which lay the top half of a humanoid figure made entirely out of metal. From its torso spilled out whatever substituted for its innards, a mess of thin tubes and fine metal wire. Its face was the most unnerving part of the whole contraption. It's eyes were perfectly round and blank, with no nose or ears to speak of. Where its mouth should be was replaced by small metal bars inlaid into its face. It lied face up, its arms falling limply off the sides of the small table. Gwen felt horrified at the sight of this metallic monstrosity, but Leon sauntered over, unfazed, and began to poke and prod at it. Shocked, Gwen cried out "Are you not disturbed at all by this thing? It's terrifying!"

"Well, I'm not sure you need to be afraid of something without legs. Besides, this is an amazing discovery! I've never heard of anyone finding a Criterion relic so well preserved. It's been thousands of years since the Criterions disappeared, and yet this thing appears to be just fine. Well, maybe not 'just fine,' but you know what I mean. I wonder what this thing was meant for?"

"Honestly, that's the last thing on my mind right now. The fact that it's shaped like a person really makes me feel uncomfortable. Let's just keep moving so that we can figure out what's down here and leave this place."

"Alright, if it creeps you out so much we'll get moving."

"Thank you."

Gwen felt better now that they were moving away from the almost-person in the room behind them, but she still felt uneasy about this place as a whole. Something didn't feel right to her. The illusion that she saw at the entrance felt wrong somehow. She was an illusion Alterer, so she knew how illusion Alterations are supposed to feel. Normal illusions are a projection of sorts. The one creating the illusion shifts the perception of the people they want to target, making it seem real only in their mind. So was there someone up at the surface creating the fake part of the forest specifically for them? It wasn't as though someone could cast the illusion without knowing they were there. So if it wasn't an illusion, what was it? As they moved down the next corridor, Gwen decided to ask Leon about it.

"Hey Leon? I'm confused about something."

"What is it?"

"The false portion of the forest that we saw at the entrance. Something about it just doesn't make sense to me. I don't think there was anyone around in the forest that was casting the illusion, so how could it be that we couldn't see the entrance?

"Oh, that. It's most likely a product of Criterion handiwork."

"Well, you've been going on about how surprising it is that this place is in such good shape. How is this place in such good condition after so long?"

Leon suddenly stopped to look at Gwen. "That's what I've been trying to figure out. Nothing in this place should still be working. The same way our magic takes energy to use, Criterion work needs energy to function. We don't know exactly how they powered their creations, but no one else has ever discovered powered artifacts before, much less a fully functional Criterion structure."

This sent a chill down Gwen's spine. "So what do you think is going on?"

"I think there's someone down here tampering with the ruins. Maybe they've figured out some sort of way to get the place back into working order. That raises another question, though. Why? What's down here that's worth all the effort, that's worth hiding? That's what we need to find out."

As they walked down the hallway and towards the next room, they began to hear a sound echoing down the passage. It sounded like metal scraping metal, and, ever so faintly, the sound of a roaring fire could be heard. The source of the noise became abundantly clear once they entered the room. Against the far wall sat what appeared to be a gigantic furnace. Metal tubes spewed out of the furnace and into the walls behind it, like the spindly legs of a horrid insect. Two long knee-high containers sat beside the burning bug. Large metal gears lined the rest of the walls, slowly turning round and around. The gears were rusted in places, and made loud scraping noises whenever the rust scraped against another gear. The smell of grease and smoke permeated the room, with the hint of something else, like the smell of burnt food, just barely perceptible beneath the other smells.

"Well, I think we know how this place is getting its energy," Leon said. He wore a face of deep thought, his brows furrowed in contemplation. "The furnace looks newer than the rest of the room. It looks pristine compared to the rusted gears. Someone must have installed this recently. This giant thing has to need fuel of some kind, so that means that someone is still down here to feed the flames. I guess my intuition was correct. That still leaves the question of why they're doing all this, though."

Gwen walked over to the chests and, with curiosity and worry in equal measure, slowly pushed one of them open. Inside sat crystals that Gwen had never seen before. They were a pale green, and they seemed to glow slightly irrespective of the light around them. "I think I found something!" Gwen called out to Leon, still deep in his own contemplation.

Leon, shaken suddenly back into reality, walked over to see what Gwen was talking about. She took one of the crystals out of the chest, and turned it in her hand, feeling its weight and running her finger along the imperfections in the crystal.

"Hey Leon, I have an idea," Gwen said abruptly.

At this, she set the crystal on the ground and took a few steps back. "I'm wondering if the crystal might be the fuel for this thing. Try setting the crystal on fire."

Leon reached his hand out and sent a little spark towards the gleaming crystal. As the spark hit, the crystal caught fire very quickly, letting off a bright white flame along with a wave of intense heat and pressure. It was as if a wave of force washed over the room, causing the pair to recoil instinctively. As the crystal burned, it began to pop and crack, sending small shards of the crystal flying off in different directions. Slowly, the light and heat dissipated, as the crystal burned to ash. "Well," Leon said with eyebrows raised in surprise, "that was a hell of a lot stronger than I was expecting. I wonder if there's more in the second chest."

Leon moved to the unopened chest and flung it open. Inside was not the glimmering crystals that they expected, but instead various pieces of hunting equipment. Traps, hunting knives, and even some pots and pans lay strewn about the bottom of the chest. Gwen moved her hands over her mouth to stifle her shock. "I think I know where those hunters disappeared to," Leon said with a grim certainty.

Gwen uncovered her mouth and, speaking just loudly enough to be heard over the din of the room, asked, "Do you think that someone killed them?"

"Well, I doubt they were just storing their gear here for the next hunting season. We'll have to be careful. Whoever is doing all of this is clearly dangerous, and they also seem to dislike interlopers poking around the place."

Gwen nodded slowly. She felt her anxiety rise even further, but she tried to push it back down. She couldn't let her discomfort get in her way right now. She had a job to do. There was once again a doorless portal on the right side of the room, leading down a seemingly identical corridor as the one they had just come from. "This place is built like a maze," Gwen observed aloud. "What kind of madman designed this place? There are no paintings, no carvings, not even any sort of furnishings for the rooms! It's all just metal and stone. There hasn't even been a single living thing besides us down here!" Gwen felt her pent up frustration at the whole ordeal rising to the surface. She felt like she was about to scream. She was used to the open air, the trees, the grass. Nothing about this place felt normal. Nothing felt safe.

"I don't know. I guess the Criterions weren't very fond of decorations." Leon's callousness hit Gwen like a slap in the face. She was mystified at just how little the whole thing seemed to affect him.

"How are you not scared? How does nothing in this place seem to even faze you?" Gwen asked incredulously.

Once again, Leon stopped in his tracks and turned around to face Gwen. "You want me to be honest with you? Nothing about this situation feels right to me. The idea that someone is fixing up old Criterion handiwork and killing anyone they find down here is unnerving to say the least. I might not be showing it, but I've been on edge since we got down here."

This comforted Gwen more than any of the jokes that Leon had made thus far. It made her feel a little self conscious knowing that even an experienced Guild member like Leon was at least a little bit frightened by everything going on.

Leon turned back around and continued down the hallway, and Gwen followed, a little bit more confidence in her stride than before. All of the hallways in these ruins seemed to stretch on for unnaturally long, but this hallway felt even longer than the rest. That same cold, unchanging light shone on them from above from some unknowable source. It felt like an eternity before the duo finally made it to the end of the passage.

The contrast between the hallway and the room they found themselves in was staggering. The hallway opened up into a spacious cavern. The floor and the walls were smooth, gray stone, with no sign of the pale bricks that lined every surface in the prior rooms. Stalactites clung to the ceiling above them, the first sign of anything natural since they left the Mistyoak Forest. All thoughts of the natural seemed to drop away in the presence of the structure in the center of the room, however. Two thick beams of metal arched out towards the cavern ceiling, rising about 20 feet from the ground. They came together at their peaks, forming into the skeletal frame of a dome, with metal bands running around the outside. From the intersection of the two arches came a bright red light that shot straight down into the earth and disappeared into a cavernous maw at its base. The sound of stone breaking apart could be heard from within the hole, and an eerie pink light shone out from its depths. More furnaces, just like the one they had seen in the room behind them, sat at the base of the structure, their tendril like pipes fed into more chests of the green shimmering crystals. The furnace's pipes then snaked up and around the arches, converging on the peak of the structure where the light was emanating from. As Leon and Gwen entered into the cavern, a figure cloaked in rose colored robes stepped out from behind one of the arches.

The figure bowed at the waist and exclaimed, "Ahh, I thought I heard voices echoing through these ancient halls! Welcome to my humble abode, although I can't say I remember inviting anyone to come over today."

Leon and Gwen both instinctively pulled out their weapons upon seeing this hooded figure. "Oh, what terrible guests you are!" the man cried out. "Threatening your host is bad manners, you know."

"Cut to the chase," Leon said tersely. "What are you doing down here?"

"My, what models of courtesy and manners my guests are! Well, if you must know, I have a little project going on down here. It's very personal, and I don't very much like being disturbed. I also don't like it when people gossip about me or my home, so I don't tend to let my guests get the chance"

Gwen yelled back angrily, "Is that why you killed those hunters?"

"Oh, you mean my prior guests? Well, I suppose they were just too curious for their own good. They stumbled into my house, uninvited, and discovered me at work. I didn't want them to go around telling everyone about what was going on down here, or else I'd never get my privacy back! So I just had to make sure that they found a place to go that wouldn't be of any trouble to me. You know, I must say that I've used worse fuel before. They burned rather nicely."

Acting in unison, Gwen and Leon charged at the figure, their weapons at the ready. "Oh no no no," the figure exclaimed as they ran towards him. "I think you need to sit down for a moment." As he said this, the figure held up his hands and pointed his palms towards the pair. Suddenly, they were blown backwards into the cavern wall behind them, as though a wind storm had surged from the man's hands. The impact knocked the wind out of both of them, and they leaned against the cavern wall for a moment, dazed and in pain.

The robed man clapped his hands in delight. "See, now, isn't that better?"

"Why are you doing this?" Gwen managed to gasp in between breaths.

"Oh, it's so nice to see one of my guests finally take an interest in my work! They normally just scream, and it honestly gets rather tiresome. I guess I may as well tell you a story. After all, what kind of host would I be if I didn't entertain my guests?" The hooded figure began to pace back and forth, his hands clasped behind his back. "A long time ago, there was a glorious goddess named

Variel. She was the source of all the magic in the world."

Gwen's mind was racing, trying desperately to think of something. "She brought the very world we stand on into being, but her children were ungrateful. They locked her away, keeping her separated from her glorious creations. Then her children were humbled by their own rebellious creations, and they agreed to work with the goddess."

Suddenly, inspiration struck. When the man's back was turned to her, she began to make quick, subtle movements with her hands, keeping her voice to a whisper. Leon looked at her with confusion, but decided that he would follow her lead. "She would help them, and in return she would be allowed to remain in Gaya, but kept deep underground, far away from her creations. Her children also agreed that, once she escaped from her prison, she could once again assume her rightful place as both the ruler of the gods and of the creatures of Gaya.

Gwen turned to Leon and motioned towards the rambling man, now pacing very quickly. She whispered, "Get behind him. Trust me." Leon nodded, and slowly rose to his feet, making his way as quietly as he could. Even when the man was looking in his direction, he did nothing to stop him.

The man was in a sort of frenzy now, gesturing wildly

with his hands as he paced. "Her chaos will wash over the world once again. She will burn this wretched world to the ground, and bring a new, better world from its ashen corpse. She promised me power, knowledge, and a place at her side if I aid in her escape, and so here I am, using the very same weaponry that humbled the gods to free my mistress from her chains." The man stopped suddenly in place, and turned to stare directly at Gwen. "Does that help you, little girl?"

"It sure does," Gwen said with a sneer.

Suddenly, the Leon that, in the robed man's mind, had been sitting next to Gwen faded from his vision, as the real Leon leapt out from behind him. He swung his greataxe down towards the figure, but he saw Leon just in time, and sidestepped the blow. Leon's axe crashed into the rocks just next to the crazed man, sending up a shower of gravel spraying in all directions.

"Vaeriel's chaos protects me!" the man exclaimed as he once again shoved Leon backwards with wind from his hands.

This time, Leon was able to stop himself before he hit the wall, and sent a blast of fire careening towards the Chaos Cultist. The Cultist swung his hand into the air, and a blade of wind shot out, parting the fireball just before it reached him.

"Vaeriel gifts me with her blessing. Your luck has run out, Alterer!"

As the Cultist stepped forward to blast Leon again, he saw a shortsword flash in front of him as Gwen stabbed towards the insane assailant. He went to blast her with his wind magic, but suddenly she disappeared from his view. The Cultist looked around him, desperately searching for any sign of her. Then, from just outside his vision, she struck at him again, this time catching him unguarded and slashing him across the side with her blade. The Cultist stumbled backwards in pain and surprise, but he didn't have time to right himself as another blast of fire shot from Leon. This time it found its mark, and the Cultist took the brunt of the hit square on. His rose robes singed at the heat of the blast, and the man clutched desperately at the burn hole at his chest.

"Enough!" The Cultist screamed. He violently flung his arms to his sides, sending out a blast of wind in all directions. It hit like a hurricane, sending Gwen and Leon up into the air, only to come crashing down hard into the stone ground.

"I've had just about enough of you two. How dare you enter my home and attack me? I have tried to be a gracious host, but you have drained me of my patience. My other guests were an unfortunate necessity, but I am going to enjoy feeding you to my machines."

Gwen slowly raised herself up to her feet. She began to make small motions with her hands, whispering words of ancient magic. As she did so, a shape seemed to split off of Gwen, and then another. As the forms began to fully take shape, two more Gwens seemed to draw their swords.

"Lies! Folly!" the Cultist cried out in fury. "No Alterer can create life! That is impossible!"

Gwen's eyes shone as the three versions of her surged forward, running circles around the Cultist. They swung their swords wildly at him, causing the cultist to duck and dodge desperately to avoid her strikes. The Cultist was steadily forced backwards, stumbling into one of the open chests feeding the insatiable furnaces.

"Leon, the crystals!" Gwen yelled out.

The trio of Gwens faded into nothing, as the real Gwen stood defiantly where she had been thrown after the blast. The Cultist realized too late what it was that he was leaning against, as one final blast of crackling flame shot out from Leon's hands. The Cultist had barely a moment to react before one crystal lit another, and another. Then, the chest began to buckle under the pressure of all this burning fuel. As the crystals sent out more and more of their fiery shards, more and more of the chests began to catch. In seconds, the chests gave under the strain, and exploded, reducing the Cultist to a fine red mist. . The force of the blasts was too much for the structure to handle, and it collapsed in on itself, crashing into the very hole that it had been digging.

Gwen fell to her knees as the whole cavern began to shake. Stalactites began falling from the ceiling all around them as Leon grabbed Gwen and made a desperate dash for the exit. Leon could hear stone crashing down around them as he dove back into the hallway with Gwen, landing prone onto the cold white brick just before the full weight of the cavern came crashing down, filling the entryway with stone and debris. Leon leaned Gwen up against the wall of the passageway, her eyelids fluttering open and closed. "Are you alright?" he asked quietly.

"Can I just take a quick nap?" Gwen responded.

Leon blinked in surprise, and then, after a second of shock, erupted into hearty laughter. Gwen unable to keep a straight face any longer, burst out laughing in turn. After a few minutes of rest in between fits of giggling and mirth, Gwen managed to get to her feet, and, with Leon's help, they both made their way back through the cold stone and metal of the ruin, before finally emerging out through the illusory trees and back into the world of the living.

The sound of chirping birds and rustling underbrush seemed like music compared to the whirring and grinding of that cold and lifeless tomb. Gwen flung herself onto the ground, lying face down on the forest floor she never knew she would miss. "I have never been so glad to see grass in my entire life!" she exclaimed with relief.

Leon leaned against one of the trees that was truly there, and Gwen sat up to look at him. "Are all Guild missions like this?" she asked. Her tone had lost the nervous edge it had taken on in the ruins, and seemed to regain the gentle curiosity it had when they began their journey.

"Not for you they probably won't be." Leon replied, staring off into the forest. "Most of the time it's just taking care of some bandits or hunting down some monsters, but as you spend more time at the Guild, they're going to send you on more and more dangerous missions." Leon turned to look at Gwen, who was looking back at him like a student eagerly waiting for their teacher to continue a lesson. Leon sighed and continued, "You know, if you want to quit now, I wouldn't blame you. You could just walk away, have a normal life. Well, as normal a life as someone who knows how to harness magic can have. You could take up a normal trade, build a house, maybe even start a family. It won't be anything glorious or adventurous, but you'll be comfortable, safe. But I think we both know that you aren't going to do that, are you?"

Gwen laughed at this, falling back onto the grass, gazing up through the trees and towards the clear sky above. "Are you kidding? After everything I've gone through? There's no way I'm quitting now." She stopped laughing, and her face took on a more serious expression. "There's way more things for me to find, more people for me to help. Who knows what would have happened if we hadn't been here to stop this maniac? I wouldn't be able to look at myself if I didn't put all of my training to some good use."

"No, no I suppose you wouldn't. People who come to the Guild are never the kind of people to back away from danger. Hell, I wasn't able to stay away either. I will warn you, though. This kind of work is draining. There's always somewhere to be, something to do. You'll barely have time to rest, and you almost definitely won't be able to settle down. I want you to think carefully about this. Are you sure that this is the kind of life you're willing to lead?"

Gwen was silent for a moment. She still stared up into the blueness of the sky above, thinking about her wants, her needs, her future. After a moment she sat up to look Leon in the eyes. "I can't stomach the idea of abandoning those in need. If I can help even one person, even if it's at some great cost to myself, then all of my training, all of my sacrifices will have been worth it.

Leon shook his head, his grin betraying the relief he felt at her answer. "I thought you might say something like that. Well, so long as you know what you're getting yourself into, I don't feel like stopping you." Leon reached his hand down to help Gwen up. Gwen took his hand, and he pulled her to her feet. He shook her hand, raising an eyebrow and giving one of his rare, genuine smiles. "I think that you are gonna be something great someday. But, before you go off to have your legendary adventures of altruism and glory, you get to come help me explain to that good for nothing mayor about ancient civilizations, goddesses of chaos, and how in the hell it all relates to those hunters."

Gwen giggled behind her hand, a mixture of pride and gratitude welling up within her. The pair of adventurers started on their journey back to the village, where they suspected no fanfare would be waiting for them this time. Gwen walked side by side with Leon, her hood resting unused at her back. She gazed straight ahead, lost in thought once again. This time, however, instead of anxious thoughts of impressing her partner, hiding her ears, and fears of botched missions, Gwen's mind raced with the possibilities that her future held. She felt free to forge her own path, no longer held back by worries of her race or thoughts of her troubles at the Guild College. She gazed around at the skittering creatures of the forest, and felt, for once, at ease.

Acknowledgements

I would like to give a heartfelt thanks to…

My parents for everything that you do for me. Without your love and support, I would never have had the courage to do this. Thank you both so much. I love you.

The whole team at Orange Hat Publishing | Ten16 Press for allowing me to intern with you, and for helping me through the whole process. You've all been an amazing help, and there's no way I could have done it without you. Thank you, Shannon, for giving me this opportunity and for setting all of this up. Thank you, Sean, for working with me to make my story better. Thank you, Jayden, for creating both the cover and the map. They turned out better than I could have ever imagined. Thank you to Lauren, Kaeley, and Jenna for taking the time out of your busy schedules both to teach me about what you do and to help make this book a reality. You all have done so much for me, and I don't think I can thank you enough.

Dr. Patrick Mulrooney, not only for your help on this project but also for all you have taught me over the past four years. You helped shape me into the writer that I am today, and your input has been invaluable during the writing of this story. I could never have done this without you.

You, the reader. I appreciate you taking the time to read my story more than I can ever express. Thank you.

About the Author

Colin J. Fantry is an eighteen-year-old high school senior at University Lake School in Wisconsin. After graduating, Colin will be attending DePaul University in Chicago, where he plans on pursuing a degree in video game design. *Chrome and Chaos: A Gaya Story* is Colin's first foray into fiction writing, and he has no plans to stop any time soon. Colin plans to combine his passion for storytelling into his video game design and hopes to create new, exciting interactive stories in the years to come.